BOOK CARD

PLEASE KEEP THIS CARD
IN BOOK POCKET

A CHARGE WILL BE MADE IF
THIS CARD IS NOT WITH THE
BOOK WHEN RETURNED.

LOS ANGELES PUBLIC LIBRARY

001389 J CH

E MAPLESON AN 005

EARS

DO NOT REMOVE FORMS FROM POCKET

CARD OWNER IS RESPONSIBLE FOR ALL
LIBRARY MATERIAL ISSUED ON HIS CARD

PREVENT DAMAGE - A charge is made for
damage to this item or the forms in the pocket.

RETURN ITEMS PROMPTLY - A fine is charged for
each day an item is overdue, including Sundays
and holidays.

REPORT A LOST ITEM AT ONCE - The charge for
a lost item includes the cost of the item plus a
$5.00 non-refundable service fee.

 LOS ANGELES PUBLIC LIBRARY

0186 11625

Anytime Mapleson and the Hungry Bears

by Mordicai Gerstein

illustrated by Susan Yard Harris

HARPER & ROW, PUBLISHERS

Anytime Mapleson and the Hungry Bears
Text copyright © 1990 by Mordicai Gerstein
Illustrations copyright © 1990 by Susan Yard Harris
Printed in the U.S.A. All rights reserved.
1 2 3 4 5 6 7 8 9 10
First Edition

Library of Congress Cataloging-in-Publication Data
Gerstein, Mordicai.
  Anytime Mapleson and the hungry bears / by Mordicai Gerstein ;
illustrated by Susan Yard Harris.
      p.   cm.
  Summary: When he meets a family of hungry bears in the woods at
the peak of maple sugaring time, Anytime Mapleson, who likes
pancakes anytime, invites them home for some pancakes and maple
syrup.
  ISBN 0-06-022414-2 : $. — ISBN 0-06-022415-0 (lib. bdg.) :
$
  [1. Bears—Fiction. 2. Maple syrup—Fiction. 3. Pancakes,
waffles, etc.—Fiction.] I. Harris, Susan Yard, ill. II. Title.
PZ7.G325An 1990   89-34473
[E]—dc20   CIP
                                                  AC

For the venerable
sugar maples of New England.
May they endure.

On the first day of March, when the fierce wind blew snow over
the rocky hills and forests of New England, the Mapleson family
got up early and Mr. Mapleson said, "It's sugaring time!"

Sugaring time is the time when the days start to warm slowly and the nights freeze up again. It is the time when the sap rises in the maple trees and starts to flow. Sugaring time is the time to make maple syrup, and the Maplesons were famous all over rocky, hilly New England for their wonderful maple syrup. They were also famous for eating pancakes.

Mr. Mapleson liked his pancakes and syrup for dinner. He was called Dinnertime.

Mrs. Mapleson liked her pancakes and syrup for lunch. She was called Lunchtime.

Their daughter liked her pancakes and syrup for breakfast. She was called Breakfastime.

Her brother, the youngest Mapleson, liked his pancakes and syrup all the time. He was called Anytime.

On this morning the Maplesons got up in the dark and frozen
dawn to get everything ready for sugaring. Dinnertime and Anytime
put on snowshoes and trudged out into the sugar bush where the
maple trees were.

They drilled little holes in all the maple trees. They put little
faucets, called spigots, into each hole. They hung a red bucket on
each spigot to catch the sap, and Anytime put a little tin roof
on each bucket to keep the snow and rain out.

When Dinnertime and Anytime got home, the whole family cleaned the big syrup boiling pan. Then they stacked firewood to cook the sap they would collect from the buckets on the maple trees. Then they sat around the wood stove and waited for the sap to start flowing. They waited for the days to warm slowly and the nights to freeze up again, because that's what starts the sap flowing.

But the days froze and the nights were worse. They waited a day and they waited a week. The blizzards came and changed to ice storms. They waited two weeks and they waited three weeks, and the ice turned to sleet and then back to snow. Every day the big thermometer out the window said "0."

"It seems as if winter is going to last a little too long this year,"
said Dinnertime one evening.

"So it seems, so it seems," Lunchtime, Breakfastime and
Anytime agreed.

On the first morning of April Anytime woke at dawn, sniffed and said, "There's something in the air." It was snowing slightly, it was blowing lightly. The big thermometer said "0," but there was something in the air.

Anytime piled out of bed.

He put on his long red flannel underwear and gray socks.

He put on his purple plaid flannel overwear and his dark-blue double-duty dungarees.

He put on his yellow hand-knitted all-wool sweater.

He put on his pea-green down jacket with the padded hood.

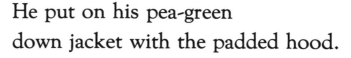

He put on his felt-lined rubber-
bottomed leather-topped duck boots,
and he put on his orange
waterproof fleece-lined hat with
the earflaps that go up and down.

Finally, he put on his greasy
gray mittens and went out into
the sugar bush.

"Watch out for bears that wake up hungry and grumpy!"
Dinnertime, Lunchtime and Breakfastime called after him.
But he was already gone.

Anytime went from tree to tree looking in all the buckets for any sign of sap, but there was none. So he kept on walking and he kept on looking, till after a time he heard a sound.

What's that sound? wondered Anytime. It was a
DRIP . . . DRIP . . . DRIP!

Then it became DRIPPETY . . . DRIP . . . DRIPPETY . . . DRIP . . . DRIPPETY . . . DRIP! and all around him the snow started melting off the trees and big chunks of it began slipping off the branches. The drops dripped down, drumming on the snow, drumming into the frozen ground, drumming,
WAKE UP! WAKE UP!
It was warming up slowly.

"Wow!" said Anytime. He ran to the nearest sap bucket, looked in, and sure enough, there was a tiny drop of sap on the tip of the spigot. It fell into the bucket, *PLINK!* and was followed by a bigger drop, *PLUNK!*

Anytime ran to the next bucket and the sap was dripping faster, *PLINK, PLUNK, PLINK, PLUNK!*

"YAY!" shouted Anytime, and he headed for home.

He hadn't gotten very far when something blocked his
path. It was small, black and furry with a bright-red head.

"Mrlf! Grlf!" it said.

It was a small bear with a sap bucket stuck on its head.

Should I help him pull the bucket off? wondered
Anytime, or should I just tiptoe past him and run home
as fast as I can?

But the bear said, "Mrlf! Grlf!" so sadly that Anytime
decided to help him. He'll probably be grateful and
friendly if I do, he thought. Anytime grabbed the bucket
and pulled up as the little bear pulled down, and *POP!* the
bucket came off.

"GRRRROOOWWLL! GGRRROOOWWWFFFF!" said the bear rudely. To Anytime it sounded like, "I'm a small black bear who just woke up from my winter's sleep and I'm cranky and hungry and you look like BREAKFAST!"

"Breakfastime is my sister," said Anytime. "Please don't eat me, friend bear. Come home with me and you can have all the pancakes and syrup you can hold."

"GRRRRFF, GGRRRRFF, GRRRFF!" said the bear, which sounded like, "Don't make me laugh! Your family won't have pancakes with a bear."

"They will if you put on my dark-blue double-duty dungarees and my pea-green down jacket with the padded hood, and I tell them you're my friend Harvey," said Anytime.

The bear thought for a moment about pancakes and syrup.

"Okay," he said. It was the only English he knew.

With the jacket and dungarees on, the bear did look a lot like Anytime's friend Harvey.

As they headed for home, all around them they heard,
DRIPPETY-PLUNK, DRIPPETY-PLINK, DRIPPETY-PLUNK!
as the snow melted and the sap flowed.

They hadn't gotten very far before something blocked their path.
It was a bigger bear with a sap bucket over its nose.

"Let's just tiptoe past and run home," said Anytime to the small
bear.

"Grrmm, grrmm," said the small bear, which sounded to
Anytime like, "No. That's my mom."

So Anytime took hold of the bucket and the small bear took
hold of Anytime, and they both pulled one way while the mother
bear pulled the other, till *POP!* off came the bucket.

"GGGRRROOOWWWLLLL!!!" said the mother bear. To Anytime it sounded like, "I'm a big black bear who just woke from my winter's sleep and I'm cranky and grouchy and hungry and you look like LUNCH!"

"Lunchtime is my mother," said Anytime, "and she makes the world's best pancakes and maple syrup. Please don't eat me, Mrs. Bear."

"He's invited us home with him for pancakes and syrup," said the small bear to his mother.

"GROWLY, GROWLY, GROWLY!" answered his mother, as if
to say, "Don't make me laugh! His family won't have pancakes
with bears."

"They will if you wear my yellow hand-knitted all-wool sweater
and my orange waterproof fleece-lined hat with the earflaps that go
up and down, and I tell them you're my friend Harvey's mother,"
said Anytime.

The bear put on the sweater and hat, and she did look a lot like
Anytime's friend Harvey's mother.

As they headed for home, all around them they heard,
DRIPPETY-DRIP, PLUNKETY-PLUNK, DRIP, DRIP, DRIPPETY-
PLINK, PLUNK, PLUNKETY! The sun shone, the sap flowed
and the snow melted. Off in the distance Anytime could smell syrup
starting to cook down at the sugarhouse.

"My dad's been collecting the sap," he said to the bears. "We'd
better hurry."

They were just about to hurry when they found something
blocking their path. It was a huge black bear with a sap bucket
stuck between its jaws.

"It's Dad," said the small bear to his mother.

Anytime took hold of the bucket, the small bear took hold of
Anytime, the mother bear took hold of the smaller bear and they
all pulled, till POP! the bucket came out of the huge bear's mouth.

"GGGRRRROOOWWWWEEEELLLL!!!" said the huge bear. To Anytime it sounded like, "I'm a huge black bear who just woke from my winter's sleep and I'm cranky and grouchy and ornery and HUNGRY, and even though you did me a big favor, you look like DINNER!"

"Dinnertime is my father," said Anytime.

"He's invited all of us home with him for pancakes and syrup," the mother bear said to her husband.

"GGRRAAHH HAA HAAAA!" roared the father bear, as if to say, "Don't make me laugh! His family won't have pancakes with a family of cranky, grumpy, ornery, HUNGRY bears!"

"Yes, they will," said Anytime. "Just wear my felt-lined rubber-bottomed leather-topped duck boots and my purple plaid flannel shirt, and they'll think you're my friend Harvey's father."

The huge bear couldn't get the felt-lined rubber-bottomed leather-topped duck boots on his feet, so he put them on his ears. And the purple plaid flannel shirt was way too small, so he tied it around his neck.

"I bet we're the best looking bears in the woods," he said to his
wife and son.

Off they went through the sugar bush, hearing, *DRIPPETY-PLUNKETY, DRIPPETY-PLINKETY, DRIPPETY-PLUNKETY!* The smell of syrup cooking was so strong they could have found their way blindfolded. Finally, they saw the sugarhouse with steam pouring out of the top, and in they went.

"Just look at you!" said Anytime's mother to him. "You went out in only your long red flannel underwear and gray socks!"

"And my greasy gray mittens," replied Anytime, holding them up and wriggling his fingers.

"We were worried about you," said Dinnertime and Breakfastime. "We were afraid you might have met some bears."

"Nope," said Anytime. "I just met my friend Harvey and his mother and father, and invited them home for pancakes and syrup."

"Glad to meet you," said Dinnertime, shaking hands with the bears. "But there's no time to talk now. We've got to keep the fire going to keep the sap cooking 'cause the syrup is almost ready."

So the bears passed the firewood to the Maplesons, who stoked
the fire till Dinnertime checked the big thermometer and said, "It's
syrup! And it's GRADE A FANCY!" which meant it was the very
best syrup.

Minutes later, the bears and the Maplesons sat at a table piled
high with pancakes and hot new maple syrup.
Breakfastime ate 50 pancakes.
Lunchtime ate 100 pancakes.
Dinnertime ate 300 pancakes.

The bears ate 1,000 pancakes and were so stuffed, they went
back to the woods and slept for another month.

And Anytime ate 1,297 pancakes. Then he drank a big glass
of milk and ate 537 more. After that, he forgot to count.